HARLEQUIN

Tempo di Valse ♩. = 60 *espr.*

& COLUMBINE

THE NUTCRACKER

Dedicated to the memory of

ERNST THEODOR AMADEUS HOFFMANN (1776–1822), *master of the fantastic, who wrote* THE NUTCRACKER AND THE MOUSE KING; ALEXANDRE DUMAS PÈRE (1802–1870), *dramatist and novelist, who retold Hoffmann's story as* CASSE NOISETTE; *and* PETER ILYICH TSCHAIKOVSKY (1840–1893), *composer and conductor, who wrote* THE NUTCRACKER *ballet.*

THE

NUTCRACKER

ADAPTED AND ILLUSTRATED

BY WARREN CHAPPELL

Schocken Books · *New York*

Waltz of the Snowflakes

First published by Schocken Books 1980
10 9 8 7 6 5 4 3 2   81 82 83 84

Published by arrangement with Alfred A. Knopf
© Warren Chappell, 1958

Music adopted from the score of *The Nutcracker* by permission
of the Tschaikovsky Foundation

Library of Congress Cataloging in Publication Data

Chappell, Warren, 1904–
The nutcracker.
Reprint of the ed. published by Knopf, New York.
SUMMARY: After hearing how her toy nutcracker got
his ugly face, a little girl helps to break the spell
and change him to a handsome prince.
[1. Fairy tales] I. Chaikovskii, Petr Il'ich,
1840–1893. Nutcracker. II. Title.
[PZ8.C3665Nu 1980]   [Fic]   80–15576

Manufactured in the United States of America
ISBN 0-8052-0660-4

IT WAS CHRISTMAS EVE. Snow was falling, spreading a soft white blanket over the old city of Nuremberg. Outside the sound of occasional sleigh bells and laughter broke the silence; inside there was expectant stillness as the last preparations were made around the tree. In Nuremberg it was the custom to give gifts on the night before Christmas, rather than on the day itself.

In the home of Judge Silberhaus his two children waited outside the parlor door with great eagerness and curiosity. Fritz was a strong and handsome boy, boisterous and willful. Marie, his delicately beautiful younger sister, had a gentle, loving disposition.

Few children in the town could look forward to a more exciting Christmas than Fritz and Marie. In addition to the presents from their mother and father, there would be those from their godfather, Doctor Drosselmayer. Godfather Drosselmayer was no ordinary doctor, nor was he an ordinary-looking man. He was tall, thin, and stooped. In his wrinkled face one eye glowed, while the other was covered by a black patch. On his bald head he wore an ingenious wig of spun glass, which he had made himself. He was a remarkable inventor,

who could make little lifelike puppets that walked and danced, performed on instruments, and drilled with guns. Some could even speak a few simple words. A glass-doored cupboard in the parlor held many wonderful toys that Godfather Drosselmayer had made for the two children.

At last Fritz and Marie heard a carol being played; then a bell tinkled, and the parlor door was opened by their mother and father. And there, in the center of the room, the splendid Christmas tree, brilliant with candles, seemed to grow from the table on which it stood. All kinds of toys, candies, and cookies hung from its branches, and they danced in the twinkling light. More gifts and toys were heaped high around the base of the tree.

Fritz saw a squadron of red-coated hussars mounted on white horses, which would be a fine addition to his large army of foot soldiers. Then he caught sight of the chestnut horse which he had wanted most of all. He mounted it happily and galloped about the room.

Marie found a doll, large and beautiful, which she named Claire. There was also an elegant silk dress, hung on a rod so that she could admire it from all sides. But her attention was quickly caught by a new figure among the toys, a little man made of wood, who seemed to be waiting his turn to be noticed. His body was too long for his thin little legs, and his head was too

large for his body. His coat was trimmed with gold braid, and on his head was a green stocking-cap. From the back of his neck a piece of wood extended, which gave the appearance of a narrow cape. As Marie studied the little man, his features expressed a gentleness and kindness to her. There was serenity in his prominent light green eyes, and cheerfulness in the smile on his bright red lips. And he had an engaging curly white beard that covered his chin.

Her affection increasing, Marie asked her father to whom the little man belonged, and she was told that he was to serve both her and her brother. Then the judge picked the little fellow up and lifted his wooden cape. As he did so, the bright red lips of the figure parted, showing two rows of white teeth. Marie was told to place a nut between the teeth, and to press on the cape. The mouth closed as she pressed, and the nut was cracked, leaving the kernel in her hand.

Hearing this cracking sound, Fritz left his chestnut horse and begged to crack the next nut. But he pushed such large and hard nuts into the little man's mouth that finally, with a cra-a-a-ck, the jaw was broken, and several of the small white teeth fell to the floor. Marie burst into tears, and insisted that she alone should have the wounded nutcracker. Godfather Drosselmayer chided her for such devotion to the homely little creature, but

Marie's mother and father agreed to put him in her care until he was strong again. Quickly she gathered up the tiny teeth, then tied the nutcracker's jaw together with a ribbon from her new silk dress.

It was late. Godfather Drosselmayer said good-night and went out into the snowy street. All the family went off to their rooms except Marie, who begged for a few more moments at the beloved toy cupboard. By the dim light from a ceiling-lamp, she tenderly lifted the disabled nutcracker into a soft bed intended for her doll Claire, and, drawing the covers up to his chin, promised to care for him and to ask Godfather Drosselmayer to attend to his loosened teeth and broken chin. At the mention of Drosselmayer's name, the nutcracker seemed to wince, and his green eyes glared so brightly that the girl was startled. But he resumed his kind expression so quickly that Marie thought she might have been mistaken, and that the sudden change was caused by the flickering light.

Marie closed the cupboard door and turned to go to her room. As she did so, the big clock, on top of which was a large gilded owl, began to make a purring sound that preceded its striking. Marie saw the owl's wings droop so that they covered the clock, and its catlike face was thrust forward. The clock was striking midnight, and as it struck, the owl took the form of Godfather

Drosselmayer, his long coat hanging down where the bird's wings had been.

Then from all sides of the room came a hissing sound. There was a scampering of tiny feet behind the walls, and bright little eyes peered out of the cracks. It was an army of mice, and it advanced toward Marie, rank on rank. Louder and sharper came the hissing, right under her feet. The floor heaved and split and cracked. And the Mouse King, with seven crowned heads, appeared before her. As the army of mice moved toward her, Marie, trembling in fright, leaned against a door of the cupboard, shattering the glass, which fell to the floor with a crash. She felt a sharp pain in her arm. At the noise of the crash the mice disappeared into the cracks in the walls again.

Now a commotion began in the cupboard. The toys were sounding a call to battle. Nutcracker threw back the covers and sprang out of bed. As he did so, the hissing began again, and the Mouse King and his army came out of hiding.

Nutcracker jumped from the upper shelf, drew his sword, and took command of his army of toys. Drums beat, trumpets sounded, and the little army descended from the cupboard shelves. They were a brave band, but they were no match for an endless horde of mice. Nutcracker was forced back again and again, until he was at the base of the cupboard. Marie could bear the sight no

The Mice

longer. She took off one of her shoes and hurled it into the midst of the battle, striking the Mouse King, and rolling him over on the floor.

At once all the fighters disappeared, the mice into the walls, the toys into the cupboard; and again Marie felt the sharp pain in her arm. She tried to reach a chair, but before she could do so, she fainted away.

SUNLIGHT was streaming through the frosted windowpanes of her room when Marie awoke. Her mother and the doctor were bending over her bed anxiously. She asked about Nutcracker, and wanted to know whether the mice had gone away. Although she described the battle between the toys and the mice, she could see that neither her mother nor the doctor believed her story. They said soothingly that she must rest, that the mice had gone away, and that the little nutcracker was back in the glass cupboard, happy and well.

Godfather's Story

THE next evening Godfather Drosselmayer came to see Marie. He sat beside her bed, and told her a story, to explain how Nutcracker and the Mouse King had become enemies.

IN a small country, not far from Nuremberg, a beautiful baby girl was born to the King and Queen. Her hair was long and golden, and her teeth pearly white. The King and Queen named her Pirlipate.

The Queen said she must be guarded all of the time, so she was watched over by six strong nursemaids who sat around the cradle, each with a cat in her lap. These unusual measures were taken because of Dame Souriconne, the Mouse Queen. Many months before the Princess was born the Mouse Queen had vowed to cast a spell on the first-born of the royal couple.

This was all because the King was very fond of sausages. When the Court Astrologer told him the time was right for sausage-making, he asked the Queen to prepare them in the way she had always done. While the Queen was in the kitchen preparing a large quantity of pork for the King's favorite dish, Dame Souriconne appeared from her home beneath the hearth. She begged for some of the meat. Out of kindness, the Queen gave her a juicy morsel. But the delicious odor attracted the Mouse Queen's seven sons and

numerous relatives, who greedily fell upon more of the pork. This commotion brought servants running with brooms and brushes, and the mice were soon driven back under the hearth. The loss of so much good meat ruined the quality of the Queen's sausages. This made the King so angry that he decided to put an end to mice.

He sent to Nuremberg for the famous Inventor Drosselmayer, who, on arriving at the palace, was told to devise some means of getting rid of all the mice there. The Inventor set to work at building a hundred little oblong boxes, each with a wire inside, to which a piece of salt pork was attached. When the meat was removed from the wire, a tiny door would close behind the thief, shutting him in. With these boxes, all the mice in the palace were caught—all, that is, except Dame Souriconne, who was much too clever to be taken in by such a simple scheme. And although the Inventor was sent away with a handsome reward, he did not know that his work was not finished. The Dame lived, and she appeared soon after to the Queen and threatened to cast a spell on the Queen's first-born child.

The threat was accomplished. One night, when the Princess was only three months old, the six guardian nursemaids, with their six cats on their laps, fell asleep. Dame Souriconne had been waiting for this moment to carry out her dreadful plan. One of the nursemaids awoke just in time to see her leaving the Princess's cradle, and she sounded an alarm. The child was crying, she was alive. But when the nursemaids looked at Pirlipate, they saw that her eyes had become bright green, her mouth reached from ear to ear, her head was too large for her body, and a small white woolly beard was on her chin.

Again Inventor Drosselmayer was sent for. This time he was told that he must break the spell or lose his head. His assignment seemed impossible, because the Inventor had but one small clue to help him: the Princess had become very fond of nuts. But by consulting the Court Astrologer, who in turn consulted the stars, Drosselmayer found that in order to break the spell Pirlipate must eat the kernel of the nut Krakatuk. The shell of this nut, so hard that a cannon's wheel could run over it without crushing it, must be broken in the presence of the young Princess by a young man who had never been shaved and had always worn boots. The kernel of the nut must be presented by the young man with his eyes closed, after which he was to *take seven steps backward without stumbling*.

The King told Inventor Drosselmayer and the Astrologer to search for the nut Krakatuk, and for the young man who could crack it. So they set out, and

for fourteen years and five months they searched the world over, without success. During these travels the Inventor lost his hair by sunstroke, and his right eye by an arrow wound. His long coat became ragged. Finally, though it meant death, he knew there was nothing to do but go back to the King and admit his failure.

Because he returned faithfully, Drosselmayer was spared death, but was sentenced to prison for the rest of his life. He begged only one favor from the King, that he be allowed to return to Nuremberg for a brief visit with his brother, a toy merchant in that city. The favor was granted. Accompanied by the Astrologer, Inventor Drosselmayer hastened to the home of his brother, to whom he described his adventures and told his plight.

When the nut was mentioned, Brother Drosselmayer remembered that he himself possessed a nut which might be Krakatuk. It had been bought under somewhat odd conditions years before, and, despite the fact that it had since been brightly gilded, never had been sold. He fetched a box, in which lay the large gilded nut. With great delight the three men discovered KRAKATUK carved on its shell in Chinese characters.

While they were rejoicing in the discovery of Krakatuk, the toy merchant's son, Nathaniel Drosselmayer, a handsome young man of eighteen,

came into the room, and there was a happy reunion between him and his uncle, the Inventor. The Astrologer studied this young man intently, and after asking him some questions he learned that Nathaniel always wore boots, that the hairs on his chin had never been shaved, and that his hobby was cracking nuts. Indeed, his nickname was "Nutcracker." This was surely the young man the stars had predicted would be able to crack the nut Krakatuk!

After a piece of wood was fastened at the back of his neck in order to strengthen his jaw, Nathaniel was dressed in costly new clothes. Then, with his uncle and the Astrologer, he went back to the little kingdom where Pirlipate waited to be rescued from Dame Souriconne's spell.

Many young men came forward, hoping to succeed in cracking the nut. All of them failed in their attempts, but Princess Pirlipate secretly hoped that the handsome Nathaniel, who was the last to try, would be successful. She was overjoyed when he easily crushed the thick shell between his teeth. As she ate the kernel of Krakatuk, she became once more angelically beautiful.

But when Nathaniel, blindfolded, took the seven steps backward, the Mouse Queen burst through the floor, and threw herself under his feet. Nathaniel's heel came down on her; he stumbled; and, alas, the handsome young man became as deformed and ugly as the Princess had been.

Instead of winning the hand of the Princess, he was ordered from her presence, and, along with his uncle and the Astrologer, he was banished from the kingdom.

At nightfall the Astrologer consulted the stars once more, and the stars foretold that young Drosselmayer, now a nutcracker, might still become a prince if he wished to be one. He could make his choice when his deformity disappeared. But his deformity would disappear only after he had overcome the Mouse King with seven heads, who was the son and heir of Dame Souriconne, and after he had won the love of a charming young lady—in spite of his ugliness.

The King
of the
Toys

WHEN Marie was allowed to get up, she went straight to the glass-doored cupboard. Nutcracker was completely restored, with all his teeth in place. Gazing at him, Marie was sure that he must be the bewitched nephew of Inventor Drosselmayer, who was none other than her own godfather. She spoke to Nutcracker softly, offering him her loyalty and affection. In return, the little man appeared to reply to her, asking her help and pledging himself to her.

That night Marie was awakened by the hissing sound that she remembered so well, and then she saw the Mouse King standing by her bed. He demanded that she give him her sugarplums and marzipan, or he would kill Nutcracker. The girl gave him the sweets. The next night the seven-headed creature came again, ordering her to surrender her sugar-and-bisque figurines to him if she wanted to save her friend. A third night he came, and it was her picture books that she had to sacrifice.

Marie finally told Nutcracker about the Mouse King's greedy demands. Nutcracker's mouth moved jerkily, and he said she must not give up anything else. If she would find him a strong sword, he would take care of their enemy. From her brother, Fritz, she borrowed a toy sword, and gave it to Nutcracker.

Lying in bed that night, too excited to sleep, Marie heard the clock strike

twelve. At the final stroke noises came from the parlor. There was a clinking of swords, a scurry of feet—then silence. Presently she heard a soft knock at her door, and a soft little voice asked her to open it. She swiftly opened the door, and there stood Nutcracker, sword in hand.

He beckoned Marie to follow him. Together, they went to a closet in the hall. From a sleeve of one of Judge Silberhaus's coats Nutcracker pulled down a little stairway. They had no sooner set foot upon the stairs than they were transported onto a perfumed meadow, which glittered and gleamed as if it were strewn with precious stones.

It was the Plain of Sugar Candy. Nutcracker led Marie through a splendid door made of orange-flower conserve, pralines, and raisins. It opened on a gallery supported by columns of sugared orange and paved with pistachios and macaroons. They journeyed on and came to the Christmas Forest, in which some of the trees were covered with snow and lit with thousands of candles. Others were hung with fruits of many colors.

Marie wanted to stop and enjoy the wonder of this place. Nutcracker clapped his hands, and shepherds and shepherdesses, hunters and huntresses came out of the forest. They were like tinted Dresden figurines that had come to life. A stool of nougat candy was brought for Marie, and then a

Andantino ♩ = 76

Dance of the
Reed Pipes

ballet was performed for her to the music of reed pipes and hunting-horns. When the ballet was over the little group of dancers vanished into a thicket.

Marie and Nutcracker walked on, past the Orange River, and came to a village where the walls of the houses and churches were made of brown marzipan, encrusted with tiny pink, blue, and white bon bons, and the roofs were gilded with icing. On they went, and came to the River of the Essence of Roses. Again Nutcracker clapped his hands, and this time a swan-shaped boat appeared, made of shells and drawn by golden dolphins.

In this boat they crossed to the City of Jam, a city of such originality and magnificence that Marie was overwhelmed as she gazed at it. Its ramparts and towers were built of *glacé* fruits, covered with crystallized sugar. As they entered the gate to the city, soldiers of silver presented arms, and a little man dressed in a gold brocaded coat ran to them, embracing Nutcracker and welcoming him to the City of Jam.

In the center of a great square stood a huge sweet bun, shaped like an obelisk. From it, fountains of lemonade, orange juice, and syrup gushed forth. Delightful little people, dressed in gaily colored clothes, filled the streets. The dazzling palace that faced the square was called the Palace of Marzipan.

Waltz of the
Flowers

dolce cantabile

pp

cresc.

f   *dim.*

Four beautiful little ladies came out from the palace to greet Nutcracker; they called him "Prince," and "Brother." They were princesses of the City of Jam, and when Nutcracker told them Marie had once saved him by throwing her shoe at the Mouse King, the princesses hailed her as the rescuer of their brother.

Then they all went into the palace to prepare and enjoy a feast. Marie felt enveloped in a soft mist; sounds grew dimmer and dimmer; she felt herself rising higher and higher. Suddenly she fell, as if from a great height, and woke up. It was daylight, and she was in her own bed.

MARIE did not tell her family about all the wonderful and beautiful things that filled her imagination. But, as the years went by, she continued to relive her adventures. She grew into a quiet, charming girl, so absorbed in her thoughts that she was often called a dreamer.

One day, when she was nearing her sixteenth birthday, her godfather was in the parlor, repairing a clock. Her mother, too, was in the room. Marie was seated near the glass cupboard, and suddenly she began to speak to the Nutcracker. She told him she would never have treated him as the Princess Pirlipate had done, because she loved him too well.

As she spoke the word love, Marie heard a step, and looking toward the parlor door she saw a young man, short and handsome, who was elegantly attired in red velvet trimmed with gold. His hair, curled and powdered, was caught in a long queue which hung down his back. In his hand he carried a bouquet, which he presented to Marie. For Fritz he had brought a sword of finest steel. The young man was Godfather Drosselmayer's nephew, Nathaniel.

At dinner young Drosselmayer obligingly cracked nuts for everyone, and afterward he asked Marie to go with him into the parlor where the glass cabinet stood. There he asked for her hand, and told her that together they would reign over the Kingdom of Toys and Sugar Candy.

The Judge and his wife gave their consent to the marriage, provided that the young couple wait a year; and Godfather Drosselmayer gave his blessing. Although the year went by very slowly, the momentous day finally arrived. Marie and Nathaniel were married in the Palace of Marzipan. It was a happy occasion, a time of feasting and dancing. And in that beautiful country where Marie still reigns with the Nutcracker King, there are as many wonders as ever, for those who have eyes to discover them.

Chinese Dance

TEXT *set in Monotype Bembo.* COMPOSED *by Westcott & Thomson, Inc., Philadelphia.* DESIGNED *by Warren Chappell and Charles Farrell.*

HARLEQUIN

& COLUMBINE